EXPERIENCED

A REAL MAN, 4

JENIKA SNOW

EXPERIENCED (A Real Man, 4)

By Jenika Snow

www.JenikaSnow.com

Jenika_Snow@Yahoo.com

Copyright © September 2016 by Jenika Snow

First E-book Publication: September 2016

Photographer: Juliana Andrade

Cover model: Wander Aguiar

Photo provided by: Wander Book Club

Editor: Editing By Rebecca / Kasi Alexander

ALL RIGHTS RESERVED: The unauthorized reproduction, transmission, or distribution of any part of this copyrighted work is illegal. Criminal copyright infringement is investigated by the FBI and is punishable by up to 5 years in federal prison and a fine of $250,000.

This literary work is fiction. Any name, places, characters, and incidents are the product of the author's imagination. Any resemblance to actual persons, living or dead, events, or establishments is solely coincidental.

Please respect the author and do not participate in or encourage piracy of copyrighted materials that would violate the author's rights.

※ Created with Vellum

He'll show her how a real man treats a woman...

SABINE

I'd never known how good it could feel to be taken care of by a man who knew what he was doing.
Until I was with Hugo...

HUGO

I was older than she was.

She was innocent, hadn't experienced all that life had to offer.

I could give her that experience.

Sabine consumed my thoughts, made me desire nothing else but her. No other woman compared to her, and because of that, I hadn't been with a woman for four years, which was also the last time I saw Sabine.

But I was done feeling guilty for what I desired. I wanted Sabine in my life, by my side, and I was about to make that a reality.

I didn't know if she'd ever been treated the way a female should ... but I was going to show her how a real man takes care of a woman.

WARNING: If you're into super short, hot, dirty reads containing a much older hero and younger heroine ... keep on reading. This story is guaranteed to make you feel all warm and fuzzy inside, give you that sweet HEA we all deserve, and make you want to search out an experienced older man for yourself.

NEWSLETTER

Want to know when Jenika has book related news, and giveaways, and free books?

You can get all of that and more by following the link below!

———

Sign Up Here: http://eepurl.com/ce7yS-/

———

1

Hugo

She's all I thought about for the last four years.

Since I left after her high school, and eighteenth birthday, celebration, Sabine had been on my mind.

Four. Fucking. Years.

I closed my eyes and pictured her.

I *always* thought about Sabine.

I could picture her long black hair ... strands I wanted to wrap around my hand as I made love to her.

I imagined her blue eyes staring up at me, wide, pleasure-filled, as I thrust into her body.

I could picture my hands, mouth, and tongue moving along her womanly curves.

Four years of me wanting a woman I knew I shouldn't desire, but whom I couldn't get out of my head.

She was so much younger than I was, but that wasn't an issue. The age difference didn't bother me in the slightest. She was a woman, twenty-one years old, and she was smart, perfect for me. Sabine had always known what she wanted out of life, and she'd excelled at what she put her mind to. I might not have seen her in years, but I knew she had only gotten more determined in that regard. That wasn't a trait someone just let go of.

I also didn't care that she was Leo's—a family friend's—daughter. Maybe I should have, but I didn't let a complication like that stop me from aching for her in a way that made it hard to think of much else.

It had been four long years since I'd even been intimate with a woman. I just couldn't bring myself to go there with them, not when the only one I wanted was Sabine.

After all this time, I knew she was the only one I'd ever want, and as experienced in life as I was, I knew this wasn't a passing desire.

I ran a hand over my face, breathing out wearily.

"Would you like something else to drink, Mr. Romanov?"

I looked up at the flight attendant and shook my head. "No, thank you, Marcella." I had three more hours to go before I landed in New York, and another hour drive to get to Leo and his wife Annabelle's house. And by the time I got to their home, it would be too late to see anyone really.

Getting a hotel would have been a simpler option, but it was out of the question, not when Leo and Annabelle insisted I stay in their guesthouse. I knew better than to argue with either of them.

I should have been here earlier.

I'd missed Sabine's graduation, and even though I'd known about this event for some time, switching my business obligations around hadn't been possible. That didn't stop me from feeling this immense guilt.

I reached into my pocket and pulled out the white leather box. Opening it, I stared down at the diamond tennis bracelet I'd bought for her.

Sabine was the only woman I'd ever given jewelry to, and although it might seem like an innocent gesture, a congratulatory gift for her accomplishments, the necklace, and now this bracelet, meant more to me than she'd ever know.

She meant more to me than she'd ever know.

Sabine

It had been four years since I'd seen him.

Four years of me wanting a man I knew I could never have.

Four years of me comparing every guy I tried to have a relationship with to him ... Hugo.

I'd told myself I needed to wake up and realize I could never have a man more than twice my age who was my father's lifelong friend.

But telling myself what I should and shouldn't want was a lot harder to accomplish when what I wanted was unattainable, yet still within my reach.

I stared across the table at my parents. We'd finished throwing a small dinner party in celebration of me graduating college with my bachelor's degree, and now it was just the three of us. I should be focusing on graduate school, getting my master's in education, but knowing Hugo was coming in tonight was all I could think of.

Hugo Romanov.

Just thinking his name had my skin prickling with awareness, had every part of me speeding up. Adrenaline rushing through my body caused this reaction.

"He'll be here sometime tonight, although I'm not sure what time."

I looked at my father. He leaned back in the dining room chair and lifted his wine glass to his lips. He looked over at my mother, who also had a wine glass in front of her.

"It's been what, four years since he was last in the States?" my mother asked.

My father nodded. "Yes, for Sabine's high school graduation. Although he came back about a year ago on business, he couldn't take the extra time to fly out to see us."

My heart sped up knowing he'd been here, probably states away, yet still closer than when he was in Europe.

"I bet you're excited to see Hugo again," my mother said and took a sip of her wine, looking over the rim at me.

I shrugged, not about to show how nervous I was, or how much anticipation thrummed through me.

We'd finished off a bottle of wine between the three of us, and the second bottle was already half empty. I reached out and ran my finger along the base of my glass. "It's been a long time," I replied softly, thinking about the last time I'd seen him. I remembered vividly the way he smelled of dark and delicious cologne. But he'd also smelled of aged books and experience, and it was such a heady, intoxicating aroma. On instinct, I lifted my hand and touched the rose gold feather necklace he'd given me. It had been a present from Hugo not just for graduating high school, but also making valedictorian.

I'd worn it every day since receiving it.

"You two always had this special bond."

I looked up at my father after he spoke. "Not really." He might have been more of a presence in my life when I was younger, and he lived in the States, but I'd never say we'd been close.

"Of course you did. Hugo would spend hours with

you at the kitchen table teaching you Russian. Remember?"

I did, vividly. Our last lesson had been when I was seventeen years old, and he'd come to visit after being away on business in Russia.

"That's because Dad wanted him to make me more 'rounded'." I smiled at my dad. He'd been teasing when he'd made the suggestion I start learning a language, but Hugo had taken it seriously. For the next two years, from the age of fifteen to seventeen, whenever Hugo was in town, he'd spend hours with me, teaching me his native language—one of the four he spoke fluently.

The truth was I could only speak a handful of Russian phrases, mainly because I wasn't able to concentrate when he was near.

But I'd tried to come to the realization that my personal reality did not include Hugo.

And even after all these years, it was still hard to make that sink in.

2

Hugo

I didn't wait for the driver to open my door. I was out, grabbed my two bags, and stood there for a second looking up at Leo's home. The porch light was on, but I had a key to the guesthouse, so I wouldn't need to disturb anyone.

"I'll let you know when I leave," I said to the driver without looking at him.

I made my way around the back and unlatched the gate to the backyard. Once it was closed behind me, I walked toward the one bedroom guesthouse. I saw the edge of the swimming pool before I rounded the corner, and the lights under the chemically enhanced water made the liquid take on a more yellow glow.

Then I saw a ripple move across the once still liquid.

Surely Leo or Annabelle weren't in the water at this hour? I rounded the corner, but stopped, seeing the back of a female body. The long, black hair was piled high on her head, and the small tie of her bikini was in a bow in the center of her back.

Every part of me froze as I stared at Sabine. I didn't need to see her face to know who it was, and I didn't need to be at her parents' house to know she was the one in the water.

I'd know her anywhere, whether I could see her face or not.

I tightened my hands on the leather straps of my bags and knew the gentlemanly thing to do would be to look away or make my presence known. Instead, I stood there motionless, silent, and watched as she now lay on her back, floating in the water. Her eyes were closed, and the rise of her breasts above the waterline had this deep-rooted need slamming into me.

My cock hardened.

My pulse quickened.

And all I wanted to do was strip out of my clothes and join her in the water.

She turned around and opened her eyes. She gasped and splashed backward when she saw me, and I felt like a voyeur for watching this clearly private act.

"I'm sorry," I said, feeling ashamed, but also feeling aroused and hot for this woman.

And she was a woman ... all curves and softness.

She wiped the water off her face and slowly shook her head. "No, you're fine. I was just startled." She offered me a smile, and that small gesture had every muscle in my body tightening harder.

This wasn't just about me wanting Sabine in my bed, under me, taking every inch of my cock.

This wasn't about me needing a younger female to make me feel alive.

This wasn't about me thinking this was some taboo desire I felt for her.

No, this was about me wanting her as *my* woman.

She was young, over two decades younger than my fifty years of age, but none of that mattered. Age was just a number.

She swam over to the edge of the pool to get out, and even though every good intention to turn and give her privacy rose up in me, I found myself standing there, watching her, and taking in every second of this moment.

The droplets of water that slid down the long lines of her body.

The swell of her breasts as they rose above the hemline of her bikini top.

The slight protrusion of her hipbones as they peeked above her swimsuit bottom.

The roundness of her ass as she bent down to grab her towel.

God, she was gorgeous, spectacular, and it wasn't just on a physical level. The slight glint of the necklace she wore caught the light, and I realized it was the feather I'd given her four years ago.

I couldn't deny that the fact she still wore it all these years later pleased me to no end.

I'd only planned on staying a few days, but I didn't want to leave, not without her.

Sabine

I felt his eyes on me as I grabbed my towel. I would be lying if I said I didn't admit I enjoyed him watching me.

I stood and lifted the towel to my face, patting the water off my mouth and cheeks, and watched him. He stood so still, his big body seeming tight. What was he thinking right now? Was he looking at me in the way I wanted him to, in the way that *I* looked at him?

We didn't speak. It was a little strange standing here with just my bikini on, at three in the morning, with Hugo watching me like he was this predator about to grab his prey. But I also liked it.

I'd missed him so much.

"It's been a long time, Sabine."

His thick Russian accent had always done something to me, something wicked and warm. He didn't look much different from the last time I'd seen him. These last four years had certainly been good to him.

"It has. I'm glad you could come."

"I wish I would have been here sooner, for the actual ceremony."

I smiled and held the towel to my body. "You're here now, and that's all that matters."

His hair was on the whiter side, with a splattering of gray thrown in. But his face wasn't aged, not like how I'd seen on other fifty-year-olds. My father certainly didn't look like Hugo.

He wore a suit, the white shirt underneath it unbuttoned at the collar, and his tanned, toned chest and neck on display. He was a large man, tall, in shape, but this air he wore about him made him attractive to me. He could look at a person and seem like he knew their entire story. He was successful, intelligent, but he was also kind.

He'd always been so kind, and I think that's why I loved him.

God, don't go there. Don't even think that with him standing right in front of you.

"You look well, Sabine."

I fought back the shiver at hearing him say my name. His accent seemed to be a little thicker when he pronounced it.

"Thank you," I whispered. I was on the verge of saying he looked well, too, but he nodded and headed toward the guesthouse. I stood there, watching his big body move fluidly, but right before he unlocked the door, he turned around and looked at me. "You should go inside. It's late, and even though this is a nice neighborhood, I'd feel better if you were safely inside."

I felt my cheeks heat at his worry for me.

"We'll talk in the morning, spend time together."

I nodded and wrapped the towel around me, and still, we stood there, staring into each other's eyes.

"Good night," I said softly, my throat tight.

"*Spokoynoy nochi.*"

I smiled. I might not be fluent in Russian, but I at least knew that one.

"*Spokoynoy nochi.*" I said goodnight to Hugo and turned before he went inside. I still felt his gaze on me when I went inside the house and shut the door.

3

Sabine

It was awhile before I fell asleep last night, but once I did, I didn't wake up until nearly ten. I blamed the activity from yesterday, and my nerves at seeing Hugo that made it difficult to settle my body.

I sat on my bed, staring out the window. I needed to find a place of my own. I'd stayed with my parents while going to school, commuting to and from campus, and saving the money I'd earned over the last four years. It had been the smart thing for me to do, but I'd graduated, and even though I was going back for my master's, I needed to be on my own.

God, I can't stop thinking about Hugo.

The exchange last night had been more awkward than normal. Even four years ago, Hugo had embraced

Experienced

me, told me how proud he was of me. But last night ... it seemed like both of us were strangers. Of course, I knew why I felt like that, because wanting him was seriously messing with me. But why had he acted so strange? Feeling his eyes on me had been thrilling, but had they meant more than just a man looking at a woman instinctively?

Was I brave enough to actually find out?

I should have been worrying about my future, about what my next steps were, but having him so close, under the same roof, played havoc with my mind and body.

I could hear him downstairs, speaking with my father, and even though his voice was muffled, a tingle shot through me. It was deep, baritone, and every part of me came alive.

After a shower and doing my hair, I went downstairs, hating that I was so nervous. Hugo laughed at something my father said, and my heart jackknifed in my chest. I rounded the corner and saw them in the sunroom, my mother just coming in with a platter of tea and pastries.

"Morning, honey," my father said, and gestured for me to come over. I looked over at Hugo, who watched me intently.

He wore a button-down black shirt, the first few buttons at his collar undone. His muscles were pronounced under the pressed, smooth material, and I willed myself not to stare. I tried to smile, but I knew it came out forced. It was just so hard, for some reason, to act like I wasn't affected.

Hugo looked relaxed, with his arm outstretched over the back of the chair. I could see the definition of his biceps, and it turned me on.

God, my parents are right here. Stop.

I took a seat beside my father, which had me sitting directly across from Hugo. He still watched me, and I felt like he was appraising me, looking right into my soul.

"Hugo wanted to take us into the city, but your mother is going out with her girlfriends, and I have a prior engagement at the office."

I didn't know what my father wanted me to say. "Okay," I said and looked between the three of them.

"We're having dinner tonight, but we told Hugo you didn't have any plans this afternoon, and you'd probably be up for a city trip."

I smoothed my hands over my thighs, the skin slightly damp from my nerves.

"Honey, are you okay?" I looked over at my mom after she spoke. "You look pale."

"I'm fine."

Hugo stared at me, this knowing look on his face.

"Well, I'll be stuck at the office all night if I don't leave now," my father said and looked down at his watch. "You know how that is, Hugo."

Hugo nodded. "Of course. We'll have dinner tonight in the city, my treat."

"I should be going, too," my mother said.

Before I knew what was going on, my mom and dad were gone, and it was just Hugo and me. The nerves I'd tried to hold back—miserably, I might add—rose up violently.

"You rested enough?" he asked, his accent still doing something intense to me. My skin prickled, my heart thundered, and my palms became clammy.

"I did." I smoothed my hands over my legs again. "I haven't slept in like this in a long time."

"You must have needed it." He reached out and grabbed his coffee cup. While taking a sip, he watched me.

"We don't have to go into the city—"

"Do you not want to?"

Of course I did. Having alone time with Hugo sounded incredible. But it also scared me a little.

"I do. But if you'd rather relax after your trip—"

"I rested plenty, Sabine. I'd like to spend time with you. I came out for a visit because of you." He smiled, and every part of me tightened. He looked good sitting across from me. In his fifties, he wore his age so damn well. And his eyes, dark, brooding, attractive, always seemed to regard me like he could read me perfectly.

"I have something for you."

I sat up straighter. "You do?"

"A graduation gift." He stood and reached into his pocket.

"You didn't have to get me anything. Flying out here was a gift enough..."

"Come here, Sabine."

I found myself standing and moving toward him. The deep command of his voice was almost my undoing.

He opened the box, and the bracelet inside took my breath away. It was a diamond tennis bracelet— and not a cheap one either ... that much was clear.

"You spent too much, Hugo," I found myself saying before I could warn myself to keep my mouth shut. I looked up and him and saw him watching me. "Thank you, I meant to say. It's gorgeous."

He took the bracelet out, and the sunlight caught the diamonds, making them sparkle like electricity traveled through them. He reached out and took hold of my wrist, and in a matter of seconds, he had the bracelet clasped. I stared down at it, the diamonds positively glowing.

"You like it?" he asked, although I had no doubts he could see on my face I loved it.

"I do," I said, smiling, and I looked up at him. "Thank you so much."

He smiled and nodded, clearly pleased with my response. He lowered his gaze to my neck, and I placed my hand on the feather necklace.

"You still wear it, even after all these years."

"I never take it off." It was true, but I hadn't meant to say that out loud.

"That pleases me to hear, Sabine."

The silence stretched between us, and although it wasn't awkward, it was ... strange. I felt like Hugo watched me with interest, something that had nothing to do with being innocent.

I certainly wasn't thinking of him as a family friend.

Could he be thinking of me as something more?

Was I losing my mind even contemplating he might be looking at me with interest?

"How about I get ready and we can leave?" I finally said, clearing my throat and rubbing my hands on my legs for the hundredth time.

"I'll have my driver here in twenty."

I wanted to tell him I could drive us, but the thought of Hugo taking control, even in this small way, sent this thrill through me.

I didn't know how I was going to act like Hugo didn't affect every single part of my body, when just standing in the same room with him had me so aroused I couldn't think straight.

4

Sabine

Hugo's driver was waiting at the curb exactly twenty minutes later. I wasn't surprised though. Hugo had power, connections, and this dominating air about him that had all other people taking notice.

We were in the back of a Mercedes and heading into the city. It was an hour's drive from where my parents lived, and even though I was still nervous, I didn't mind this alone time with him.

I looked out the tinted window and watched as the city came into view. I could see the skyscrapers in the distance and wondered exactly what we planned on doing. Hugo hadn't exactly told me anything, just that we'd be spending most of the day here.

Experienced

"You didn't eat anything before we left," Hugo said, and I glanced over at him.

"I wasn't hungry." And I hadn't been, but at that moment, my belly started to grumble, giving away that I was now.

"How about we have some breakfast?"

I nodded and smiled. "Okay."

He nodded, the expression on his face satisfied. "We'll stop at Vellaim's Café first," he said to the driver.

"Of course, Sir."

Hugo looked at me again. "Then I thought I'd take you shopping."

That had my eyebrows lifting clear to my hairline, I was sure. "Shopping? For what?" The tennis bracelet on my wrist felt heavy, although I knew I mainly felt like that because I was hyper aware that Hugo had given it to me.

"I'd like to get you something nice for dinner tonight."

I didn't know what to say, although my first reaction was to decline. He'd already flown out to see me for my graduation, bought me this tennis bracelet that probably cost a fortune—a years' salary of what my parents made combined, and here he was trying to buy more for me.

"I—"

"I'd prefer if you didn't decline, because it would please me to do this for you, although I'll respect your wishes."

I stared at him, wanting this man so much I ached in

places that should have embarrassed me. But I also *wanted* to please him.

"You look shocked."

"I am," I said honestly.

"Is it that hard to believe that I want to do something nice for you?"

I shook my head instantly. "Of course not. You've always been kind and generous. But you've already given me the bracelet, and come all the way over here—"

"Because I wanted to; I wanted to make you happy." He leaned in a little closer, and I smelled the masculine scent of his cologne as it consumed me. "And I want to do this as well, Sabine."

How could I say no? He looked at me like he was ... hungry for my approval. "Okay," I whispered, suddenly feeling lightheaded and out of breath.

He smiled, this confident expression on his face.

But as the seconds moved by, and we held each other's gazes, I felt the air shift around us. It got hotter, thicker, and I felt as if I was falling into the abyss.

But I anticipated the fall.

"How's work?" I asked, my voice low, heavy sounding.

He didn't speak for a long while, just watched me, these emotions playing in the depths of his eyes. "It keeps me busy."

I nodded and licked my lips. I didn't miss how Hugo lowered his gaze to watch the act. My heart thundered harder. "You've always been so busy." God, my voice was so tight, my arousal shifting inside of me until it was as if another being resided there.

"Aside from you and your family, my business is the only thing of significance I have." He shifted on his seat, and I wanted to look down and see if he was aroused. I had no idea why I desperately wanted to see, but that need overrode everything in my brain, making me almost feel like I was malfunctioning.

"I'm glad we have this day to ourselves."

I looked into his eyes, his accent moving over me, making my skin tighten and my inner muscles clench in need.

"You are?"

He shifted on the seat again, moving a little closer to me. "I am."

"Why?" God, was that my voice sounding so aroused?

"Because it gives us some time to talk, to be alone."

I felt so dizzy, but in a good way. "You want to be alone with me?"

Yes, he just said that.

He took a second to answer. "I do, Sabine. So much." His voice was just as thick as mine.

God, is this really happening?

I felt like this was a prime time to kiss him, or for him to lean in those extra few inches and kiss me. I wanted to, wanted to feel his lips on mine, feel that power, that experience I knew he had deep in his marrow. I wanted it to fill me.

He leaned in another inch, and I found myself doing the same. For a second, we breathed the same air. His body was so big, so muscular, that he seemed to block out everything behind him. I felt wholly feminine right now, and I wanted more.

And just when I thought I'd finally feel his lips on mine, and finally get a taste of the man that I'd wanted for so long it sucked the very life out of me, the car slowed.

"We're here, Sir."

I felt reality slam into me, and as I leaned back, I was aware of Hugo still watching me. He looked at me with heavy-lidded eyes, his focus trained on my mouth. His broad, defined chest rising and falling a little harder, faster told me he was still in that moment.

I hadn't imagined this; I wasn't the only one fantasizing about being together.

Hugo wanted me as much as I wanted him.

Hugo

I was hard, painfully so. All I wanted to do was kiss Sabine right then and there. Of course, the timing had interrupted what I knew would have eventually happened. As much as I wanted to say fuck breakfast and just admit what I wanted with her, I gathered my self-control and helped her out of the car.

What I knew without a doubt was that Sabine wanted me, and I wasn't going to back down now that I'd seen the truth coming off her in waves.

She'd be mine.

5

Sabine

We'd left the coffee shop half an hour ago, but with the traffic and the fact that Hugo wanted to take me to this ritzy, exclusive boutique, we'd just arrived five minutes ago.

But already I was in a dressing room, the woman working the floor shoving dresses at me. She'd been very friendly with Hugo, but I hadn't seen it as sexual, or even attraction on her part. She'd been pleasantly surprised to see him.

I thought about Hugo's profession, about what would happen if I were involved with him. It might be wishful thinking, and I supposed I needed to be realistic, but it was hard not thinking about the *what ifs*.

With him owning his own business, he traveled a lot,

going to different countries, making deals to further his business; he had connections that made my meager life look dull and unappealing. But he'd always been a facet in my life, and I couldn't see myself not having him there. He'd always been there, even from afar. Hugo had always shown me it didn't matter how much money someone did or didn't have ... if they were genuine they were valued.

And he was as genuine as they came.

I turned and looked at myself in the mirror. For a second, I didn't even recognize myself, not with the expensive dress draped over my body, showing off my curves in the most tempting ways.

Yes, I admitted I looked nice in this dress, beautiful even, and a part of me felt uncomfortable with that fact. I didn't dress up, and when I did, it certainly wasn't with lace and silk.

Will Hugo think I'm beautiful?

I smoothed my hands over the cream colored material, the lace beneath my fingers smooth, yet slightly raised. The V-neck was right above my breasts, and the large swells gently rose above it with every inhalation I took. I only stood there for a few moments before I heard Hugo clear his throat. My heart started racing harder, knowing he was right behind the dressing room door.

"You're well in there?" he asked, and I looked myself over again. The lace detailing had rose-colored threads throughout it, and the material fell to my knees. It was classy, yet revealing without being obscene.

"I'm good," I said, but immediately cleared my throat as my voice sounded thick. The arousal still thrummed through my veins.

"You're dressed?" he asked, and I heard the distinct change in the pitch of his voice. It got lower, huskier, and I wondered if he was imagining me without anything on.

The car ride played through my head again, and I felt my cheeks heat. Looking at my reflection, I saw my cheeks had this rosy glow to them.

"I am," I said softly.

There was a moment of silence.

"Let me see you, Sabine."

My pulse jackknifed, and I felt my throat tighten. I looked down at myself, knowing I wanted to show him, because I thought I looked nice in the dress, but I felt so nervous. I'd never felt so ... pretty.

"Sabine." He said my name deeply, with a touch of authority.

I reached out and grabbed the handle and, for a second, just held the little brass globe in my hand. It started to warm when I finally pulled the door open. Hugo stood just a few feet from me, this air of confidence and control surrounding him.

He looked so damn good.

I felt my cheeks heat even further, but prayed I didn't look like a total twit. I didn't want him thinking I was embarrassed by this moment or his generosity. I also didn't want him to think I couldn't control myself and the clear attraction I'd felt between us in the car.

And God, had I felt it. I still couldn't wrap my head around the heat that had consumed me at the way he'd looked at me. He didn't speak for long seconds, but he was definitely appraising me.

"It's too much, isn't it?" I felt my hands start to shake from my nerves. I was losing it, but I couldn't stop the energy moving through me.

"*Krasivitsa.*"

I felt butterflies take root in my belly at the way he called me beautiful. It was only one word, but it sounded like he meant so much more with it.

"You're absolutely beautiful, Sabine."

I felt my damn blush intensify. "Thank you." I saw the woman holding up a few more dresses, but Hugo waved her off.

"I love this one. I think this one will be perfect for tonight." He looked up at me after scanning my body for several seconds. I liked that he took charge. I loved this dress, but hearing him shut any other dresses down, and telling me this was the one, made me feel very feminine ... very happy that he was pleased.

We didn't speak for long seconds, and I wondered if the woman still standing in the background felt weird just watching us. Surely she could see the connection that was going on? Or maybe I was the only one that felt it?

"We need some privacy," Hugo finally said, addressing the woman. She was gone a second later. I ran my hands down the dress, but caught myself and curled my fingers into fists. Hugo took a step closer and another and another, until he was right in front of me, just a few inches separating us.

I had a hard time breathing with Hugo's scent filling my head. He glanced down at my lips, licked his own, and exhaled roughly, as if he was having just as hard a time as I was.

"There are a lot of things I want to say right now, Sabine." He still stared at my mouth.

"Say them," I whispered, not caring if anyone could hear us.

"They aren't proper," he said and took another step closer to me, so much so that if I inhaled our chests would brush together.

"I'm past proper, Hugo." I was feeling bold, braver. "I know what happened in the car wasn't just one sided."

He was still looking at my mouth. My heartbeat filled my head, and I grew dizzy.

"No, it wasn't just one sided."

And then he leaned in, pushed my hair aside, and said softly against the shell of my ear, "It's always been you, and I'm tired of waiting, Sabine. I'm ready to make you mine."

6

Hugo

I couldn't stop thinking about Sabine and the moments we'd shared in the car and at the boutique. I could have taken her right then and there, shown her what I wanted to do to her, and not given a shit if the sales associate saw it. I'd been hard, so fucking hard I'd thought about going to the bathroom to relieve myself to try and tame some of this need moving through me.

But I knew nothing would compare to Sabine. I knew nothing could tame my arousal unless it was *she*.

I'd waited four years to be with her, hiding my feelings, not sure if telling her what I wanted, and hoping she felt the same way, would work out. She was an adult, knew what she wanted in life, and the way she'd reacted to me today told me she wanted me.

My driver pulled up to the house and everyone exited. I watched as she climbed out of the car, her long legs unfolding. The heels I'd insisted on buying because they matched the dress and screamed "fuck me" looked incredible on her. My cock jerked, but I tried to keep the desire that burned deep inside of me at bay.

"Thank you for dinner. It was lovely," Annabelle said and wrapped her arms around Leo.

"My pleasure." I should have said more, how it was lovely to catch up with them, how we needed to do all of that, but my focus was on Sabine and the way she wouldn't make eye contact with me. She'd been doing that all night, and a part of me felt like a predator wanting to grab onto its prey ... and Sabine was *my* prey.

I could tell she might be conflicted about what was going on between us, the arousal that I knew she felt just as strongly as I felt for her. I looked at the feather necklace she wore. It had meant so much more than just a graduation gift all those years ago. It was a token of my feelings for her, light, easily held in the hand, but complex even if on the outside it didn't appear as such.

And the bracelet she wore on her delicate wrist. I was possessive of Sabine, without a doubt, but I was also controlled, careful, and knew how to keep myself in check. I didn't even want to think about her with anyone else.

She was mine, and I wanted to show her how good we'd be together.

Sabine

After we arrived home, I'd hoped to spend time with Hugo. My parents had gone to bed a little over an hour ago, and here I was still in the dress Hugo had gotten for me, not wanting to take it off for some reason.

I didn't know what any of this meant, or if I'd even get to talk to him about it before he left, but the very thought of him leaving and not coming back for so long—however long that might be—had this sick feeling consuming me.

I didn't want anyone else. I'd known that before I'd even seen the desire for me in his eyes. The very thought of not being able to tell him the truth, to be honest with the both of us, made it seem as if the world would crash down around me.

I thought on that for several minutes and came to the conclusion I couldn't just hope something like this happened again.

Hugo was it for me.

Thinking about being with anyone else just didn't do it for me. I wanted only him, and he needed to know that.

Hugo

I've never been the type of man to sit around and wait for things to fall into my lap. I didn't get where I was in life, and with my corporation, by not taking action.

I'd waited long enough to be with Sabine, and I wasn't going to wait anymore.

But when I opened the front door of the guesthouse, I saw her standing there. She still wore the dress I'd bought her, and this stab of possession slammed into me. I wanted her wearing the things I bought.

I wanted to be the one to peel what she wore off.

Lust slammed into me, but so did love. I fucking loved Sabine, more than I could even fully comprehend … more than she'd ever fully know.

For her I'd go to any lengths to make sure she was protected. I'd level buildings if it made her happy.

"Hugo." She whispered my name, and everything in me tightened. "I'm just going to say this because I'm done hiding."

I curled my fingers into the doorframe, trying to refrain from pulling her into the house and making her mine. I wanted to kiss her until she was breathless, until she was clutching at me and begging me to make her mine in any way I saw fit.

But I didn't move, because she clearly had something

to say. This would be a break it or make it situation. She'd either tell me whatever between us couldn't go on or she'd finally give herself to me.

She looked down at her hands, which she started twisting together. She was nervous, and I hated that I'd made her feel this way, even inadvertently.

I reached out and placed one hand on hers and lifted her head up with a forefinger under her chin. She stared up at me, her eyes so wide, her expression so vulnerable.

"It's okay," I said softly, wanting to pull her into my chest so badly, to stroke my hand over her hair, and to let Sabine know she'd never have to feel anything but comfort and safety around me.

"I love you, Hugo." Her eyes got even wider when she said those words, and if possible, my body tightened even further. I let go of her hands and chin, staring at her with probably a little bit of shock on my face. However, what I felt so strongly it could have knocked me on my ass, was possession.

She's mine.

7

Hugo

"I love you so much, Hugo. I have for years. I know what I felt from you today when it was just us, and I'm tired of trying to pretend that this might go away ... that my emotions for you will diminish over time." She looked at me for a long second. "It only grows stronger as time passes."

I didn't have any self-control when it came to Sabine. Right now, the way she looked at me, the things she said ... I wasn't about to try and stop myself from having her, from showing her I loved her as well.

I couldn't have stopped myself even if I'd wanted to.

I cupped my hand on the back of her head, held her in place, and leaned forward. For a second, all we did was stare into each other's eyes and breathe the same air.

"Kiss me, Hugo," she whispered, begging me in that softly sweet voice of hers.

I groaned, my body shaking. "*Lyubov moya.*" I whispered the endearment, knowing she'd understand the Russian term. I opened my eyes and saw she understood me clearly.

She looked up at me with wide eyes.

"My love," I said on a harsh groan. "I love you, too, Sabine. God," I groaned and closed my eyes for a heartbeat. "God, I fucking love you so much it hurts sometimes." I leaned down to kiss her like it was the last time I ever would.

But it wasn't. Fucking hell it wasn't. We were just getting started.

She moaned for me, and I kissed her harder. I tightened my hold on her hair, tilted her head back, and moved my mouth down her neck. With my tongue and lips, I ran a path down the slender arch of her throat, licking, sucking, and making her know I loved every part of her. I sucked on her collarbones, loving the way she arched her back, her breasts pressing firmly into mine.

"That's it, *Krasivaya.*" I sucked on her flesh until I knew it would be red, until I knew my mark would be on her. "I've wanted you, too, for years, Sabine. I've wanted you until it's only been you consuming my thoughts, until it's only you that I've lived for."

"Hugo."

The way she whispered my name had my cock jerking. "Tell me what you want and it's yours."

"I need you. Just you."

I pulled her inside the guesthouse, shut the door, and cupped the side of her face. I ran my tongue along her bottom lip, tasting the sweet flavor of her mouth. God, she was perfect. I curled my hand around her neck even more, dug my fingers into her hair, and pulled her impossibly closer. There wasn't any part of her I didn't want touching me.

She pulled away and I moved back, giving her space.

"Are we doing this?" she asked. Her voice was soft, her lips red and glossy.

"I want to do so much more," I said in a low voice, looking at her mouth, still holding onto her.

The silence stretched between us for several seconds, and then she rose on her toes, wound her arms around my neck, and kissed me like she needed me to survive.

I groaned, loving that she opened her mouth wide for me. I plunged my tongue into the warm, sweet recess of her mouth.

"I'm so wet."

The sound of her whispered words had my cock jerking even harder. I wanted to be buried inside of her, to feel her pussy milking my cock.

I wanted to pump my seed deep in her body, make her mine.

"Is this crazy?" she asked, and I pulled back and

looked down at her.

I wanted to tell her it didn't matter if it was because this felt right, good. I stroked my finger along her cheek instead. "Maybe it is crazy, but I can't stop now that I started." I'd let the floodgates open when it came to her, and I was not about to close them.

"You can't stop?" She lowered her gaze to my mouth, and I looked at the pulse beneath her ear that was beating rapidly.

"No." I looked back at her face. "I don't want to stop."

She breathed harder. "Good, because I don't want you to stop, Hugo."

I groaned at her words. I had no control over my actions anymore, not right now, and not with Sabine so responsive to me. "*Krasavitsa*." I moved my thumb to her mouth and slowly around her pink flesh.

I looked in her eyes.

"I've always wanted you," she whispered.

I leaned down so our mouths were only inches apart. "It's always been you for me, Sabine."

She arched her chest, pressing her breasts against me.

I gnashed my teeth together at how good that felt. I turned us around and walked her backward, using my much bigger body as leverage to get her to do what I wanted.

"Do you want me?" I asked in a low, deep voice.

"Yes," was all she said.

I ran my tongue along her lips, and she parted for me.

"Do you want me to worship every part of you? Do you want to come for me?"

She shivered in my embrace and closed her eyes. When she nodded, I felt the heat from her body slam into me.

"And I would, Sabine." I pulled back and waited until she opened her eyes and looked at me. "I would worship every single part of you with my hands, mouth, and tongue. I'd make you come without even being inside of you."

She groaned.

Sabine was my undoing ... always.

"I don't want to hold back anymore, Hugo."

I reveled in the smoothness of her skin and felt like the world was crashing down around me. For years I'd held back, buried my desires, but no more. Tonight, I would show Sabine what she meant to me. I'd show her with my body how much I cared about her ... how much I loved her. I'd move heaven and earth to please this woman.

She stared into my eyes, and I felt my heart beat a little faster at the vulnerability I saw. God, did Sabine know the power she held over me?

"Touch me, Hugo," she whispered. She pressed her breasts more firmly against my chest.

"It's you and I, Sabine." And then, before anything else could be said, I kissed her again at the same time I lifted her into my arms and carried her into the bedroom.

8

Sabine

I speared my hands in Hugo's hair, tugged at the strands, and made these small noises in the back of my throat. I couldn't help it, couldn't even try and stop, or at the very least, tame my desires.

I didn't want to.

He carried me into the bedroom, and once I was on the mattress, I looked up at him. I wanted this, had dreamed about it. But I also wanted to be honest.

"I've never been with a man, Hugo." It was hard getting those words out. At twenty-one, I'd been on plenty of dates, but I'd never had actual intercourse, never even desired to with any other man.

What and whom I wanted was right before me.

"I'm a virgin." Would that turn him off?

Instead of saying we should stop, he used his upper body to push me back on the bed. He covered me with his hardness, cupped the side of my face, and kissed me. With his tongue in my mouth, he fucked my mouth the way I wanted him to do between my thighs.

I moaned again, feeling like I couldn't even control the most basic of my actions.

I felt like the world fell away, like there was nothing but this one moment in time. Whatever happened afterward, this was worth it.

He pulled away. I wanted my clothes off faster than he probably did. I rose up and raised the dress up and over my head. I reached behind me and undid my bra, tossed that aside, and finally looked at Hugo. He was leaning back, staring at me with these hooded eyes. His arousal was clear on his expression, but also in the way his pants tented out in the front.

He looked huge.

God, what would it feel like to have him inside of me?

I shivered at my thoughts.

"The panties, Sabine. Take the fucking panties off."

His voice was deep and husky, and his accent seemed thicker.

I shifted so I was braced on my back, lifted my lower body, and started taking the panties off. He watched me the whole time, his eyes half-lidded, his massive chest rising and falling.

Once those were off and I was totally bared for him, I rested back on the bed, my legs closed, my heart racing.

"Spread, Sabine." He lifted his gaze up my legs, over my breasts, and looked fully at my face. My nipples were hard, my pussy so wet I wouldn't be surprised if the sheets were slightly damp beneath me.

"Let me see you bared for me."

I licked my lips and spread my legs. My pussy was bared, my lips parting. But he still stared at my face even though my thighs were wide, my pussy on display for him.

"Do you want me to look at you?" God, his voice could make me come on its own.

"Yes," I whispered.

"Ask me then."

My throat felt so tight, like there was a lump in the center of it. "I want you to look at me between my legs."

"Show me." He still stared into my eyes, and I slowly moved my hand down my belly to the top of my pussy.

I might not have ever had sex, but I'd been touched, kissed, licked by men. It had been a lackluster experience every time, but I knew this time would be different. I knew, this time, I'd finally reach that peak I always knew I'd find with Hugo.

When my hand was on my pussy, I slowly spread my fingers through my folds. The pleasure was instant, but it was also because of the way Hugo looked at me ... watched me.

He lowered his gaze to my hand and watched what I was doing for long seconds, and I felt myself build higher to that intense pleasure I knew I could get with him. But in the next instant, he reached out and took hold of my wrist. He lifted my hand to his mouth, inhaled deeply, and this deep, almost animalistic sound left him. His gaze held mine as he licked my fingers clean, making sure that no drop of my pussy cream was still on the digits.

"I knew you'd taste this good," he said and leaned in an inch so our faces were so close I could have risen up and kissed him. "I knew you'd be this sweet."

He lowered his gaze to my mouth, and I thought he'd kiss me—hoped he would. But instead, he pulled back and took hold of my ankle. While maintaining eye contact, he lowered his mouth to my foot, ran his tongue along the arch on the underside, and groaned deeply. He almost closed his eyes, but they were still open, watching me, seeing my reaction.

Hugo started running his tongue over my anklebone, moving his lips over my calf, and going higher until he reached my knee. He shifted his hand, smoothing it along the inside of my thigh, but not touching the part of my body that wanted him the most. He kept going, licking, kissing, and gently sucking at my flesh until he made his way to my hipbones.

I was a liquid mess for him, so ready to feel him stretching me that I would have begged if I'd been able to find my voice.

He kept moving up my body, teasing his tongue around my belly button before gently dipping it into the small indentations and moving upward. When he got to my breasts, he cupped both mounds in his large hands, pushed them together, and started licking and sucking at the stiff peaks.

"Am I making you feel good, Sabine?"

I could only nod, but realized he wasn't looking at me, and instead lavishing attention on my breasts.

"Yes," I whispered.

"Good, because this is about you and making you feel good."

I couldn't breathe, couldn't even think.

"This will always be about you."

9

Hugo

I wanted to show her what a man could do to her, what *I* could do to her.

I wanted to show Sabine how good I could make her feel, that with me she'd never want for anything, not even the physical aspects.

I wanted her, was about to have her body, but I wanted her heart, as well.

I paid special attention to her breasts, making the tight skin at the peaks red and wet from my ministrations. She was panting and moaning, and I broke away, needing to swallow her sounds, take them into myself.

This was what I'd wanted from the moment I realized I couldn't let her be with anyone else, that I wanted her as mine.

Her heart.

Her body.

Her passion.

Staying away for all these years had been the hardest damn thing I'd ever done in my life.

I cupped her face and smoothed my thumb along her bottom lip until it popped out slightly. "I've wanted you since your eighteenth birthday, Sabine, since you graduated high school." I stared in her eyes, letting her know this was serious; this was the truth and reality.

"Our age difference doesn't bother you?" she whispered, her mouth slightly parted, her sweet breath moving along my cheek.

"Age is just a number, and you're the one that makes me harder than fucking steel." I ground my cock into her leg, proving my point. "From the moment I realized I wanted you," I smoothed my fingers down her neck to rest at the feather necklace, "I haven't been with another woman in years." I looked into her eyes to gauge her reaction. "I haven't wanted another woman, Sabine."

She was breathing harder. She looked so fucking gorgeous, the raven fall of her hair spread out over my pillow like spilled ink.

"The only woman I want to be buried inside of is you." What I wanted was her under me and giving herself over so there was no doubt she was mine. "Now that I have you, that I know you want this, I'm not letting you go." And I fucking wasn't. "You're mine, Sabine."

I moved my thumb along her bottom lip again, transfixed by the sight of me pulling the soft, pink flesh down.

"I want to be yours. I've always been yours."

Yeah, she fucking had.

The vulnerability and innocence on the surface of her face slammed into me fast and hard.

"You know I'll take care of you." I didn't state it like a question.

"Yes," she whispered.

"You were mine before I could even accept it myself, Sabine."

Her breath hitched, and I leaned down and took her mouth in a kiss again.

It wasn't soft, wasn't gentle. I gave her what we both needed. I listened to her soft moans, her verbal and nonverbal pleas for more. All I wanted to do was make her feel fucking incredible.

Once I claimed her, fucked her until she couldn't even walk straight tomorrow, she'd be mine. I couldn't stop until she knew she was mine.

After several seconds, I broke the kiss, needing this to go further than what we did now. Her lips were swollen, red, and wet.

"You're the only thing that fucking matters, Sabine." I slipped my hand behind her head and gripped the base of her skull. "This can be so damn easy." My mouth was still close to hers, but I didn't kiss her again. I felt her breasts against me. They were big and round, and my cock gave a mighty jerk. I pressed my dick against her again, letting her feel the stiffness of it, letting her know the ten inches that would be buried in her cunt in a matter of minutes.

"I'm going to make you feel so fucking good, Sabine."

"Hugo... be with me already."

I growled out low. "I'm going to show you how a real man takes care of his woman."

"Kiss me again."

I did just that.

Our tongues slid along each other, frantic, heated, and full of need. I was hard, so hard for her that I found myself grinding my erection against her inner thigh, needing some friction.

She was pliant in my arms, pressing her breasts against my chest, her nipples hard, her arousal coating the air. I felt drunk for her.

She lifted her hips slightly, her pussy rubbing along my leg. I needed to get undressed, to be just as bare as she was. I shifted from her and started undoing the buttons of my shirt. I tossed the material to the floor once it was off and stood up to work on my pants. My cock was hard, aching, and I needed to have the fucker free ... needed to have it deep inside of Sabine.

Once I was just as naked as she was, I grabbed my cock and started stroking myself, just looking at her laid out for me. She licked her lips slowly and lowered her eyes to my cock.

"That's it," I murmured. "Watch as I fucking jerk off because I can't control myself." It turned me on knowing she watched. "You want these ten inches in you, Sabine?"

Her eyes were slightly wide, and I couldn't help but feel a surge of pleasure at that fact.

"I could take every part of you right now." I moved a step closer. "And it still wouldn't be enough. It'll never be enough." I gave my cock one more stroke before letting the hard, thick, and long shaft go. I moved back onto the bed and curled my fingers against her side. There might be marks in the morning, but I wanted that brand of ownership, that slight discoloration that would let me know she was mine.

And I'd be the only one that saw them because she was mine.

"I don't want any other male looking at you, Sabine," I whispered against her throat. "I don't want them touching you, even if it's innocent."

She moaned and arched up into me.

"These little bruises that might show up..." I added a little more pressure to her hips, loving that she grabbed my biceps and dug her nails in. "These little marks will be for my eyes only, because you and I will both know how you got them." I pulled back and looked down at her. "We'll know that our passion was too fucking great."

She nodded slowly, and I looked down at where she had her nails in my bicep. I'd have marks, too, it seemed, and God, did that turn me on. My dick punched forward even harder. I moved my mouth to the base of her neck, and I felt her pulse beating rapidly. I licked and sucked at the spot, drawing the blood up to the surface and marking her there, too.

I wanted her screaming my name as I filled her with my huge cock.

"I want to go further, baby. I want to be so deep in you we are one."

"Don't stop." She slanted her mouth on mine and speared her tongue between my parted lips. She acted desperate for me, and fucking hell, was I desperate for her. I reached between us and palmed my cock. The tip was slick with pre-cum. I wanted it inside of her, coating her in my scent and seed.

"You're so gorgeous ... so mine, Sabine. All of you belongs to me." I placed my fingers on her lips. "This is mine." I went lower and touched her breasts. "These are mine." I kept my focus on her eyes, and I slid my palm down her belly, finally touching her soaking wet pussy. "*This* is mine."

She arched her back slightly, involuntarily.

"I need all of you." I was at my breaking point. "*Christ*, baby—" I gritted the words out. I moved my mouth to her ear and whispered, "I need to be inside of you ... now."

10

Sabine

There's no turning back now.

He pressed his body fully against mine, all hard muscle and sinew lined up with my softness. I couldn't stop thinking about the way he had touched himself. He was huge, bigger than I thought was even possible. My pussy muscles were still clamping down hard, clearly trying to find something substantial to grip onto.

His huge ten-inch cock.

He was tall, muscular, and the light sprinkling of salt and pepper chest hair above his defined pectoral muscles told me of his experience in life. This was turning out to be everything I'd thought of and wanted over the years.

I didn't care if he was over two decades older than I was, and I didn't care what anyone thought.

I deserved this.

I deserved to be happy.

I couldn't breathe, couldn't even think straight, and when he moved his hand between us, I felt like I'd come just from a touch to my clit.

"I need you, Hugo," I whispered, all but begging.

"I want you so much. Desperately, Sabine," he said against my neck, licking, sucking, and leaving his mark on me. He apparently liked my throat, but I didn't mind, because feeling his teeth, tongue, and lips on me, on any part of my body, had lights flashing before my eyes and heat consuming me.

Beads of perspiration covered the valley between my breasts. His cock was like a steel rod between us, pressing against my belly. I could feel the pre-cum at the tip spread across my flesh, and as if I'd projected my thoughts, Hugo leaned back and looked down at my abdomen. He used his fingers to spread his cum along my flesh, rubbing it in.

"I want you to smell like me." He lifted his head and looked at me. "I want to pump deep inside of you, fill you up with my seed, and watch as it starts to come out."

All I could think about was our hot, sweaty bodies pressed together as he fucked me, as he showed me what a real man did with a woman.

He lay back on me, his chest to mine, his cock now

nestled between my pussy folds. He gripped my chin tightly, holding me in place as he mouth fucked me. There was no other way to describe it. The way he pressed back and forth against me, his cock sliding between my slit and bumping against my clit had me gasping and on the verge of coming.

"That's it, *lyubov moya*." He went a little faster, pumping his cock against me, and making me utter all these explicit noises for him. "*Christ*, you're so damn primed for me." He let go of my chin and slid both of his hands behind me to grip my ass. He squeezed the mounds tightly and pulled me impossibly closer to him as he kept stroking his dick through my cleft.

When I moaned, he grunted and held onto my ass even harder.

"*God,* please, Hugo." I didn't care that I was begging, that I sounded desperate. Right now, I just wanted to feel him pushing into me, stretching my pussy, and claiming every inch of me.

Even though I was unbelievably wet for him, I knew when he finally pushed that huge cock into me it would be tough. He was just so big, and even if I weren't a virgin there would be a lot that had to stretch to accommodate him.

I was looking forward to it, needed it like I needed to breathe.

But I wanted to feel so full I couldn't stand it, couldn't even breathe.

"Are you ready for me?" he asked in that deep voice of his.

"I'm so ready for you."

"I need you so fucking much."

He kept one hand on my ass and moved the other between our bodies, took hold of his cock, and placed it at my entrance.

"Kiss me," I whispered, needing his mouth on me when he shoved deep inside.

He didn't make me ask a second time.

Hugo rubbed his cock along my cleft, up and down, not penetrating me like I wanted him to. "You're so wet for me, so ready for me." He looked right in my eyes, not stopping his ministrations between my legs.

I felt my slickness slip from my pussy and slide down my inner thigh. While he kissed me, I grabbed onto the back of his head, pulled at the strands of his short hair, needing him as close as he could get.

Groans spilled from both of us.

For years, I'd imagined being with Hugo. But I chalked those dreams up to nothing but fantasy.

But we were here now together. Our skin was sweaty, pressed together, and the idea that I was about to have sex with the man I loved made me breathless.

I was at the point I wanted him shoved so deep inside of me nothing else mattered.

He stilled above me, his muscles strained, taut. "There's no going back from this, Sabine."

I just shook my head. "Good."

I shifted, my lower half lifting up and pressing against his shaft. He hissed.

"I'm ready."

He placed the tip at my entrance again, and in a swift move, buried a few inches into me. I felt the stretch and burn start to take root. For a moment, time seemed to stand still. There wasn't any confusion about what was going to happen.

Right now there was only us.

He thrust his hips forward, pushing another inch into me. Hugo groaned and closed his eyes. "You're so tight." He pushed yet another inch into me, and the burning, stretching sensation took hold even more.

My inner muscles clenched on their own.

He grunted. "God, Sabine. You can't do that or I'll come too soon." He rested his forehead against mine, and we breathed together. "You feel so good." In one swift move, he was buried fully inside of me, and I gasped at the sudden action. "*Christ.* Just like that, baby." He started moving in and out of me, faster and harder, claiming every inch of me. I closed my eyes when it became too much to keep them open.

"Look at me. Watch me, Sabine."

I gasped when he hit something deliciously good inside of me. I opened my eyes and stared right into his. He was so far inside there wasn't a part of me Hugo wasn't touching.

He started moving again, and the sound of flesh slapping together was so erotic, so filthy, I could have come from that alone.

I love you so much.

The root of his cock rubbed against my clit every time he slammed into me.

He pushed fully into me, stilled, and rotated his hips, causing a different kind of sensation to fill me.

"*Sabine.*" He gritted my name out. "You're so tight it's almost painful." His expression was fierce. "But it's so fucking good." Sweat beaded his brow, and he made this low sound when he pulled out and then slammed into me especially hard.

"God. *Hugo.*"

"I want you to come for me. I want to *see* you get off." He reached between us and pressed his thumb to my clit, rubbing the bud back and forth while he still tunneled in and out of me.

Hell.

His breathing was short, hard pants. I knew he was close to getting off, too.

"You're mine," he said so low, almost feral. He slammed into me again and applied more pressure to my clit until I was about to explode for him. But before I went over the edge, he stilled.

I wanted to scream.

"Tell me you're mine."

That's all I've ever wanted.

"Tell me," he demanded.

"I'm yours."

He thrust in and out of me like a madman now, faster and harder. I got lost in the sensation.

He was groaning as well, an auditory pleasure that filled me.

"Fuck, yes, Sabine. You're mine, only mine."

"I'm only yours." I gasped when he slammed into me so hard I moved up an inch on the bed.

The pain only heightened my pleasure.

He started whispering in Russian to me, and that made me hotter. And I came for him, just like that.

"God, Sabine." He thrust deep in my body and stilled, his huge body tense above me, his muscles rigid, defined.

I couldn't take my eyes off him. Seeing Hugo get off was so arousing, because *I* was the one who had done this to him. I could feel him come, could feel the hard jets of his seed filling me. He was so big and warm inside me that those sensations had my pleasure mounting even more.

He thrust deep in me once more, stilled, and his haggard breathing told me everything I needed to know.

When several moments passed, he opened his eyes and looked me in the eyes. Sweat covered his brow, and I reached up and smoothed my finger over a bead. I felt droplets slide down my temple, surprising me, but also arousing me. Hugo leaned down and ran his tongue along the side of my head, licking the sweat away. When he pulled back, I felt dizzy, drunk, and so damn euphoric right now.

"Are you okay?"

I nodded. "I'm more than okay."

And I was. God, I was.

11

Hugo

Three days later

I could see how nervous Sabine was, and I knew part of it was because she thought I was leaving.

At first, I hadn't planned on setting a departure date, simply because I'd used this time to recoup from traveling. But I also knew I couldn't stay at Leo and Annabelle's house for an indeterminate length of time.

But I did not intend to leave her, not after I'd made her mine.

I cupped Sabine's face and leaned in to kiss her. I didn't deny the proprietary desire to mark her in front of whoever the fuck saw rode me strong. Leo and Annabelle where just a few feet away, and after we'd told them of our relationship, and I explained I wasn't going to stop seeing Sabine, even if they disapproved, they seemed to accept what was happening. They were unconformable about it at first. I could give them that, could understand it, too.

I was so much older, and I was a family friend. But I didn't give a fuck about any of that. They were my family … but Sabine was my life.

Sabine. Was. My. Life.

"Are you sure you want to come to the city with me?" I had no issues throwing her over my shoulder like a caveman staking his claim. But I wanted her complete devotion.

And when I looked into her face, into her eyes, I knew I had it.

"Wherever you want to go, whatever you want to do, I'll follow you."

I cupped her face in my hands and leaned down so we were eye-to-eye.

"But your work, your travels."

I shook my head. "It's my company. I'll do whatever I please, and if that means being here with you while you go back to school, or you coming with me and traveling, so be it. I can work from anywhere. I won't lie and say I may not have to travel on occasion, but my life is yours, Sabine." I smoothed my fingers along her jaw. "This is about you, about us, and I'll make it work." I kissed her again, swiped my tongue along her bottom lip, and wanted her to know this was the truth. "You're my life."

And she was, every aspect of it.

"You know I want to be with you."

I felt this surge of pleasure and testosterone move through me.

We were staying in the city alone for the next few days. I would work out my schedule, switch things, rearrange appointments, and make this work.

Failure wasn't an option when it came to Sabine.

"I want this to work, Hugo. I'd never ask you to change for me. Where you go, I go. I'll make this work, too."

I smiled, feeling so fucking happy right now.

"For me it's just you, Sabine."

There was nothing else in the world that mattered more than the woman in front of me, and I was going to spend the rest of my life proving that to her.

Sabine

We'd just stepped into the hotel suite Hugo had reserved for the next few days. He'd told me he'd work out his schedule so he didn't have to travel so much. But the truth was I didn't want him to change for me. I could finish a lot of my graduate degree online if need be.

But I wasn't going to worry about that right now. Hugo was here with me, we were together, and things would work out.

I wouldn't allow it not to.

This was my life and what I had always wanted.

I watched as Hugo went into the kitchen and got a couple of glasses out of the cabinet, and a bottle of wine from the fridge. I took that time to look at the hotel room. It wasn't standard, of course, but more of a suite, with the small kitchen, living room area, and a private bedroom down a short hallway. I walked over to the floor to ceiling windows and looked down at Times Square, which was right below us. The area was crowded with people. From this high up, it looked like a flow of colorful ink along the ground.

I felt Hugo step up behind me, his body heat seeping into me and sending this shiver racing up my spine. He didn't even have to touch me and I was affected. When I heard glass lightly clanking, I looked down to see him setting the wine glasses, now filled with ruby red liquid, down on the small table beside us. I started to turn around, but he placed a hand on my lower back, stopping me. Nothing was said as he pushed my hair off my neck, pulled my shirt down to expose my shoulder, and proceeded to kiss my bared flesh.

I placed my hands on the cool glass, closed my eyes, and just absorbed the feeling of Hugo kissing and licking my flesh. I was already so wet for him, and I felt my nipples stab through the material of my shirt. It was hard to breathe as he placed a hand on my waist and pulled me back. I felt the hard outline of his cock along my lower back, and a soft moan left me.

Still we said nothing, but words didn't have to be spoken for this moment to be loud.

He lightly sucked at my skin, the little spot where my neck and shoulder met. A wave of pleasure slammed into me, and I moaned again. Curling my nails against the glass, I leaned forward and rested my forehead on it. I wanted so much right now, and it all had to do with the man currently making my knees feel weak.

He clenched his fingers along my hipbone and pulled me even closer to his erection.

"Hugo..." I whispered.

He didn't say anything in response, just licked, sucked, and gently bit my flesh. The hand not holding onto my waist was now in my hair, lifting the heavy fall of the strands and holding them at the crown of my head. He alternated between both sides of my neck, running his tongue along the flesh, teasing me, tormenting me. But still he said nothing. He just touched me—almost innocently, but so erotic in the same breath.

And when I couldn't take it anymore, when I was about to beg him to take me, he pulled away, turned me around, and held my throat in a loose, controlling, and arousing hold. He kissed me like my life depended on it, and at that moment it did.

"I love you, Sabine," he said against my mouth, and my heart jumped to my throat.

"I love you, too," I whispered back.

He went to his knees in front of me, pulled my pants and panties down, and tossed them aside. I took a deep breath in, placed my hands behind me, palms flat on the chilled glass, and let this man—my man—pleasure me. Hugo looked up at me, his focus trained solely on me, and I had no doubt I was his world. It was the look in his eyes, the devotion I saw on his face that told me I was it for him.

Without saying anything, he lifted my leg, bent the knee, and placed it over his shoulder. I was spread for him, my weight resting on the glass, my focus on this man. And without any more waiting, Hugo leaned forward and ran his tongue up my cleft to my clit. A groan spilled from me, he grunted deeply, and I felt the world fade away.

But I forced my eyes to stay open. He pulled away, but a line of saliva came with him. I nearly came right then at the sight.

"This will always be about you, Sabine." He licked me again, right through my center, and a shiver worked its way through my whole body. "It'll always be only about you until I take my last breath."

And I knew he meant that, just like he was it for me.

12

Hugo

One year later

I couldn't keep my eyes off her, but then again that had been the case for years. She was still all I thought about, all I wanted in my life. Even if we'd known each other for years, I anticipated spending my life with her.

She looked out the window of my private jet, thousands of feet above the ground. I had business in Russia, and since it was a break from her graduate studies, and she'd never been to my home country, I thought it was the perfect time to bring her with me.

"You look especially beautiful today, *lyubov moya*."

She turned and faced me, the smile that could light

up a fucking room shining right at me. "Thank you." She looked me up and down, as much as she could since I was seated. I shifted in the leather seat, feeling my arousal grow the longer she stared at me. "You're not hard on the eyes either."

My cock jerked something fierce at her comment.

"Come here," I commanded.

She stood, the pencil skirt she wore molding to her long legs. I knew what her ass looked like in the tweed, how the roundness and curve of it showed off her perfection.

She was perfect to me. Every part of her made just for *me*.

When she was standing right in front of me, I was tempted to tell her to lower to her knees, but I wanted to please her. Making her feel good brought me an immense amount of pleasure.

I wrapped my hand around her waist and pulled her forward. She lost her footing and had to place her hands on my chest. Our mouths were close, our breath mingling.

"The flight crew could come to the cabin at any moment," she whispered, and I could hear that she didn't much care for that. I reached across the console and pressed the service button. In a matter of seconds, Marcella, my full-time flight attendant, came into the cabin.

"Something I can help you with, Sir?" She was professional, not missing a beat or acting surprised that I had Sabine nearly on my lap.

"I want privacy. I don't want anyone coming into the cabin until I specifically call for them."

"Of course, Sir." She was gone a second later.

"I have no doubt Marcella knows why you want an empty cabin," Sabine said softly, her focus on my face.

"I have no doubt she does, too." I clenched my hands into fists as my arousal grew for Sabine. "Does it turn you on knowing there are a handful of my employees just beyond that door?" She didn't respond, but her breathing increased. "Does it make you wet to know they are very aware of what I am about to do to you?"

Sabine swallowed, her pupils dilated, and she made this soft sound in the back of her throat.

"Would you like me to find out for myself?" I challenged.

"Yes," she whispered.

"Pull your skirt above your glorious ass, Sabine." She straightened, but I stopped her with a hand to her hip. "You left the panties at home, right? Just like I instructed?"

She nodded slowly, and I watched her cheeks turn a pretty shade of pink.

I sat back and got comfortable as I waited for her to pull her skirt up. She didn't make me wait long.

Lifting my eyes to look into hers, I could see she'd

pulled the material up, but I made sure to look at her eyes.

When she stopped moving, I slowly lowered my gaze. Her pussy was bare of any hair, and her slit was a gorgeous peach color. My hand twitched, the need to reach out and run a finger down the cleft riding me strong. I noticed she kept glancing at the door. "They won't enter without my specific instruction. They won't disobey me." She turned her focus to me. "Just like you won't disobey me, right, Sabine?"

She licked her lips and nodded. "I have no desire to disobey you."

"Then place your foot right here." I patted the empty leather space between my legs. She lifted her leg and placed her foot where I wanted, and I reached out and placed my hands on her knees, prying them open as wide as they'd go. She reached up and braced her hands above to balance herself. I let go of her knees and started undoing the buttons of her blouse. I stopped when only a few at the bottom were still secured. I just wanted access to the large mounds of her breasts currently being held back by transparent pink lace.

"*Christ*, Sabine." I lifted my eyes up to her face. "Pull the cups down and let your breasts spill free."

She was panting now, her face a mask of pure, unadulterated lust. She did as I said, and once the large mounds were freed of the constricting material, we both groaned. I wanted to lick at her nipples and see if they got harder, but first I wanted to lick at her pretty cunt until she came for me.

I pulled her cunt lips apart, saw the pink center, and couldn't stop myself from leaning in and licking my fill. She tasted sweet, musky, and all mine. I ate her out until her legs started to shake, and I knew she was about to get off. I doubled my efforts, wanting to be inside of her when she came, but I knew I could get my woman off more than once.

I moved my mouth to her clit, started to suck that bud with vigor, and hummed low. "Come for me, baby."

And as if my command was her undoing, she came. I didn't stop my ministrations until she was almost sagging against me. I rose up to suck on her breasts, licking and nipping at her nipples. I could have gone all fucking night, but I needed inside of her too badly.

I rose fully, turned her around so she was pressed up against the side of the plane interior, her upper body arched forward and her lower half popped out. I smoothed my hands over the curved, perfect mounds of her ass and exhaled roughly.

"This is going to be fast and hard."

She looked over her shoulder at me. "Good, because I can't handle slow right now, Hugo."

I cursed in Russian, started undoing the button of my slacks, and then pulled my zipper down. I placed my hand on the center of her back, keeping her in place, and used my other hand to reach inside my fly and grab my cock. I stroked my dick a few times while I stared at the roundness of Sabine's ass. Pre-cum already dripped out of the slit at the tip, a testament to how worked up I was for my woman.

I took a step closer to her, smoothed my hand on her back lower until it was on her ass cheek, and spread the flesh apart. I leaned back and looked at her pussy hole, slightly open for me.

"Fuck me, Hugo."

I snapped my gaze to hers, my groan just about spilling from me. She couldn't say that to me, not unless she wanted me to paint the cheeks of her ass white with my cum. I've always tried to be a gentleman when it came to Sabine. I've made love to her, got her off, and when I was too far gone, too over the edge in my lust ... I've fucked her.

That's what I was going to do now.

I pushed her legs apart wider, this feral sensation breaking free inside of me. This wouldn't be slow, wouldn't be easy, and wouldn't be gentle.

I grabbed my cock, placed it at her entrance, and looked up at her. She had her head turned to the side. Her mouth was parted, and her eyes were closed. There was a light sheen of sweat starting to cover her spine. I leaned forward and ran my tongue up the length, tasting the salty sweetness and grunting in pleasure.

In one powerful thrust, I buried myself deep in her body.

We both groaned and I stilled, my dick so far inside of her our pelvises touched. Her pussy contracted along my cock, and I reached out and took hold of her hips, digging my fingertips into her flesh.

"You're mine," I said without thought and started moving in and out of her.

"Oh. God." She moaned the words out. I watched as she bit her lip, pulling that pink flesh between her straight white teeth.

I wanted to do that, to bite hard enough she bled and then came on my dick.

I started really pounding inside her, any gentle side of me gone. She cried out and threw her head back, her long dark hair a wreath of pin-straight locks down her back. I smoothed my hand up her back and took hold of those strands, wrapping the locks around my fist.

"*Hugo*," she cried out. I had no doubt the flight crew could hear us, but I didn't give a fuck.

In fact, I got harder knowing they could hear me fucking my woman.

My balls drew up tight, but I didn't want to come just yet.

You can't hold off.

"Hugo ... I'm coming," she cried out even louder.

Hearing her say that was my undoing. I had no self-control left.

I pulled my head back enough so that I could watch myself tunneling in and out of her pussy. I saw how slick my dick was from her pussy juices, and I gnashed my teeth together in pleasure.

It was so damn hot.

When I felt her pussy contract especially hard around my cock, I couldn't stop myself from letting go and getting off.

I buried myself all the way inside her on the third powerful thrust and leaned forward to rest my forehead on the center of her back. I filled her body with my cum, bathed her in it ... marked her with it.

When I had nothing left to give her, I pulled out and looked down at her pussy. I saw my seed start to slide out of her.

She might be on the pill, but I still wanted my cum inside her. I gathered the seed slipping down her inner thigh and moved it back to her pussy, pushing my finger and the fluid back into her.

She gasped.

"Every part of you is mine, and I'll prove how worthy I am of claiming the title until the day I die." I pulled her skirt back over her ass, helped her stand up straight, and turned her around. Once I had her bra adjusted and her shirt buttoned up, I lifted her easily into my arms and sat back down. It felt good to just hold her, to know she was mine.

I'd have no problem doing that for the rest of my life.

———

Sabine

Hugo held me gently in his arms. He ran his hand over my back, kissing the top of my head. I stayed in that position for long moments.

I started to move, because I had to be heavy for him, but he just pulled me back down and held me tighter.

There was nowhere else I wanted—needed—to be.

"You're my life," he said softly against my hair.

I'd never tire of hearing him say these kinds of things to me. In the last year, I'd focused on my graduate studies. With Hugo having to fly to different countries for his business, we didn't get to spend as much time together as either of us would have liked. But every single moment he wasn't working he spent with me. He lavished me with attention, made sure to tell me every day how beautiful and special I was to him, and each day, I fell more in love with him.

"I love you," I said and wrapped my arms around his neck, making my body as flush with his as I could.

"And I love you."

As my body cooled, relaxation took its place. I settled into the gentle, protective embrace Hugo wrapped me in.

I'd never known what it could feel like to be touched, held, and loved by a real man ... until I was with Hugo.

EPILOGUE

Sabine

Six years later

I sat on the hospital bed, the gown I wore too big and hanging off my shoulder. I stared down at my hand. It was swollen, my fingers looking thick and round. I couldn't wear my wedding ring, hadn't been able to after the fifth month of pregnancy.

"She looks like you, *lyubov moya*," Hugo said as he held our daughter. "*Krasavitsa*." He looked up at me, and the pure joy on his face was priceless. "She's beautiful, Sabine."

She was. She really was. With a head of black hair and delicate little features, she was the light of our lives, and she'd been in this world less than twenty-four hours.

Hugo rose from the chair and came over to me. He sat on the edge of the bed, leaned down to kiss Bella, our daughter, on the forehead, and then handed her over to me. For long seconds, he did nothing but stare at me as I held Bella.

"What?" I asked, smiling up at the man I loved ... my husband.

He shook his head slowly. "Nothing, my love. I just am enamored at the sight of the woman I love holding our child." He leaned forward, lifted my face up with a finger under my chin, and kissed me soundly. "My life," he whispered, and that same warmth and tingling sensation I get, even all these years later, filled every part of me.

"I love you," I whispered, and Hugo kissed me on the top of the head. There was a knock on the door, and a second later my parents were coming through. I was thankful they understood my feelings and desires for Hugo, but the truth was even if they hadn't approved of it, I would have still been with Hugo.

I couldn't hold back or put my life and desires on hold based on what others thought, not even my parents.

But, it didn't matter, because they loved me and were happy that I was happy.

Hugo had waited for me to finish with my schooling for marriage and a family. He respected my decisions, supported me, and now we were ready to take the next step.

We had taken the next step.

I was his. He was mine. And together, we were it for each other.

I loved this man and the tiny creation we'd made, and he loved us. And in life, that was what really mattered.

The End

EXPERIENCED HOLIDAY BONUS
AGE IS JUST A NUMBER WHEN IT COMES TO LOVE

Sabine

I could have watched the man I loved and our daughter play dolls and have tea parties all day long.

Hugo sat on the ground, a small pink plastic table between him and our two-year-old. Our little girl spoke in Russian to him, her voice tiny, and her words hard to make out if you didn't listen carefully.

I loved that Hugo was teaching her his native tongue. I wanted her to experience all that life had to offer. I wanted her to know where her roots came from and embrace them.

The little boy I carried kicked wildly, and I placed my hand on my rounded belly. At eight months pregnant I was ready to have baby Anton. Hugo came in with Bella in his arms. He wore a too-small tiara atop his head, and a tiny red lip print on his cheek thanks to Bella getting into my lipstick earlier. I couldn't help but laugh as I took Bella from my husband and brought her over to the highchair to eat dinner.

I was about to turn and grab the plate of food I'd prepared for her, but Hugo was already on it.

"Sit, *lyubov moya*. I'll feed her while you rest."

I sat in the chair across from them and smiled as I watched Hugo lay out the cut food for Bella. She played with it for a moment before finally starting to eat.

"You're okay?"

I looked at him when he spoke. I had my hand on my belly, and rubbed it while I smiled. "Yeah, just tired."

"You do too much around here."

I liked staying busy. Hugo was such a big help around the house, and he'd since cut back on his work schedule. Unless it was a family trip, he only left out of country once a year. Maybe that was still too much for some, but compared to his schedule before it was an astronomical adjustment.

"You need to let me do more around here, although you're so stubborn." He smiled and gave me a wink. "Bella definitely takes after you in that regard." Just then Bella threw a cut-up piece of food at him. We both laughed.

When she was finished eating and was down for a nap, Hugo came back into the kitchen. He helped me off the chair and together we went into the sunroom. It was cold out, and the snow was starting to fall. We sat down; the room was heated so it wasn't like an icebox.

For long moments we just sat there, Hugo having his arm around me, and nothing but the beautiful silence, and the love of my life holding me close.

As the years progressed and our lives had changed for the better, I realized a lot of things. Without love in your life you'll always be missing something. Without that positive energy, and the feeling of being someone's world, that puzzle piece would always be absent. At least these were the things I realized for my own life. They were things I wouldn't change, and what I wished I'd come to understand sooner.

He was older than me.

We came from different backgrounds.

Our relationship may not have been typical or conventional.

And in the beginning outsiders looking in had seen our relationship as "wrong."

But in the end none of that mattered. We had our daughter, a little boy on the way, and we loved each other more than anything else.

What was important was he loved me and I loved him, and our family gave their support. Everything else was just background noise that needed to be tuned out.

Hugo

Two months later

The smell of freshly baked cookies and honey ham filled the room. I stared at my wife, the most beautiful woman in the world, and felt like the earth opened up and swallowed me whole.

How did I get so lucky?

This was how I felt each and every time I looked at her.

She sat with her mother and father, and Bella on the floor playing with her new Christmas toys. I looked down at my sleeping son in my arms.

He was so tiny and fragile, and a little piece of Sabine and myself.

The wonders of this world never ceased to amaze me.

Bella called out for me, the Russian I taught her making me smile. Her little toddler voice made the words sound sweet, even when she screamed out in a tantrum. Sabine answered her, the Russian my wife knew making me feel pretty fucking proud.

"Go see Daddy, honey," Sabine said in English this time.

Bella came over, her new doll hanging from her grasp. She stared down at Anton, her little face pinched in confusion. When she lifted her hand and stroked the dark hair atop his tiny head, I smiled at her.

"You're so sweet, *lapochka*." I leaned down to kiss the crown of her head. I picked her up and set her on my lap. Bella rested against my arm, and I saw how tired she looked. I started singing her and Anton a Russian lullaby. It was one my mother used to sing to me when I was a child. I was aware of gazes on me, and lifted my head to see Sabine and her parents watching me. The smile on my wife's face made the entire room light up.

I wanted my wife with me. I wanted her close, wanted to smell the sweet scent that always surrounded her.

I wanted the other half of my soul with me, and the little ones we'd create to stay right by me no matter what.

Sabine's parents left twenty minutes later, and when my world sat beside me I instantly leaned over and kissed her. She took Anton from me when he started getting fussy, and I adjusted Bella in my arms. My baby girl had fallen asleep, but I wasn't ready to put her to bed. I watched as Sabine undid her shirt to feed Anton. I wrapped my arm around her and pulled her in close.

There was nothing more important to me than the three people in this room. I'd make sure that there was so much love in this house we suffocated from it.

I was complete, but only because of them.

ABOUT THE AUTHOR

Want to read more by Jenika Snow? Find all her titles here:

http://jenikasnow.com/bookshelf/

Find the author at:

Newsletter: http://bit.ly/2dkihXD

www.JenikaSnow.com
Jenika_Snow@yahoo.com